Bla

Rain Stavros

Special thanks to all my friends
for support and
information without which this book
would not exist as it is.

Prologue or two

Midnight. The closest town was so far away that the glow of its streetlights was nowhere to be seen. A waning crescent moon and thousands of stars that accompanied it illuminated with their dim light a factory building in the middle of nowhere. Officially it was abandoned, so no lights were lit inside it, but someone knew that that building was in a lot more active use than it seemed.

Looking at the rooftop, it was possible to see a silhouette of a woman. She just stood there and didn't move a muscle. Her short blazing red hair was flowing in the wind and her eyes shone like amethysts, looking at something far away and at the same time not focusing on anything. She was waiting for something... or someone.

Suddenly a man opened a door leading up to the roof. He shouted something at the woman, took out his gun and pointed it at her. That was the last thing he ever did.

***

Black Iris. That name was known by everyone from mafia to Interpol. The true identity of the person behind the name was unknown. Their gender was also a complete mystery. One thing however was for sure: Black Iris was a real person and an extremely dangerous one.

During the last few years, many deaths had come to the attention of the police. They seemed completely unrelated at first glance. Poisonings, shootings with everything from a pistol to a sniper rifle, stabbings, accidents, and even apparent suicides or natural deaths.

The victims' ages were all over the map. Some still had their lives ahead of them, while others were waiting for death to knock on their door. Some of the cases would not have been investigated, had it not been for a single piece of evidence found on all crime scenes: An Iris Chrysographes or a black iris left near the body.

That flower was the only evidence there was. This is why the criminal was called by its name. Somehow a person responsible for hundreds of murders had managed to avoid surveillance cameras and photographers and no witness has ever stepped forward, for obvious reasons. Twelve of the victims had been either in witness protection or in solitary confinement.

So how did the killer choose his victims? Some officers think that the victims were randomly chosen from newspapers or from population register, but the truth couldn't be more different. You see, Black Iris did not choose the victims. They were told whom to kill and how, and he were well compensated for it. This feared and sought after serial killer was the best contract assassin in the world. If you knew how to contact them, she would kill anyone for you – for a price.

Chapter 1

The sun rose above the British Isles, colouring the earth and the sea with its red hue. People were waking up, some because of the sunlight and some because of the ringing of an alarm clock, and everyone was preparing to start off their day, following their typical routines to a T. Dogs were pulling their owners out of beds, and those who had no pet woke up later and either drove themselves to work or used public transport to get there. It was an ordinary Tuesday.

21-year-old Diana Sullivan, however, was not among those waking up. She hadn't slept a wink for three days in a row because of her job. She was on her way to her workplace to report the successful completion of her assignment, get her pay, receive her next assignment, and then sleep for twenty-four hours before getting right back on the job.

That was the life of someone working in the grey area of the law. Or should that be pitch black? The job paid well, but it had to be done without any sort of insurance regarding health or safety. The boss could also make you run around non-stop for a year and there would be nobody you could complain about it to.

But Diana didn't mind. She had been born into the profession and didn't know another lifestyle. Going freelance did sound appealing from time to time, since she would no longer have to listen to her boss nagging all the time and she could pick your own assignments.

In Diana's job however, it was a bad idea. If one weren't part of a larger organization they'd either be impossible to contact, or get caught by the law enforcers in no time at all.

You guessed it. That beautiful red haired woman is the world most wanted, and least known criminal: Black Iris.

Diana stepped into a building that appeared to be just a normal office building, which it obviously wasn't. Although the above ground section of the building housed a completely legal joint-stock company, the building had nearly ten secret underground levels, and there was a totally different kind of organization pulling the strings there. The joint-stock company of course knew nothing about it.

Diana flashed her ID cards to a security guard who let her in no questions asked. She walked to a lift and pushed the button leading to the lower parking lot, and the lift went down two floors, to the lowest official level of the building.

Diana found it irritating that it was so troublesome to get to her workplace, but one couldn't be too careful.

After getting to the parking lot, one had to walk across it to the other side of the building, press the right wall tile three times within two seconds to open a hidden door, step into yet another lift and press a button that's purposefully hidden behind the mirror just to go down one floor. Afterwards it was possible to use any of the stairs and lifts available to get to any desired floor.

And that's not all. The lift leading from the parking lot to the secret level had a camera and a computer with a powerful facial recognition software hidden behind its mirror. That computer was connected to the lift's power source.

If a person the software didn't recognize were to step

into the lift, or they were to press the wrong button, the power source would shut down, and the lift would not move anywhere before the appropriate people arrived at the scene, and I guarantee you it's not the lift repairmen.

During a power outage, it would be impossible to arrive at the workplace. Although the backup generators would allow the opening of emergency exits to let the "staff" out, those doors could only be opened from the inside.

Diana stepped into the room labelled "Dressing room, Women". She had to "fix her outfit". It was a safety policy that no one should speak to the boss while in disguise. The policy serves absolutely no purpose however, as we'll soon find out.

Diana took off her reddish brown long haired wig, revealing an ever redder short hair underneath. She put the wig into her locker, washed her hands, and took out a small two compartment casing, looking into the mirror. This was the part she hated the most about her costume.

She leaned closer to the mirror and took out her brown contact lenses, showing the real colour of her eyes. They were like amethysts. No wonder she always wore a disguise outside the base. Almost unnaturally blood red hair and purple eyes would most certainly attract attention, and no one outside the Organization should know her true face.

After putting the contact lenses into the casing and the casing into her purse, she headed to her boss's office. She waved to some of her coworkers on her way there. Her face showed no emotions. This was all just a routine and had nothing to do with having a social life.

Diana knocked on her boss's door three times and stepped through the door without waiting for permission to come in.

"Good morning Iris. Confident as always, I see", the boss, Nigel Ramirez, said to her. It had not been a complement. Nigel used the word "confidence" as a way of saying "don't push your luck". Diana paid no attention to the gesture. She couldn't care less about what her boss thought of her. She walked to Nigel's desk and dropped five folders in front of him.

"Exactly as the clients ordered. Two poisonings: One got an overdose of his own insulin, made to look like a self inflicted accident, no evidence was left behind. The other ingested enough arsenic to drop an elephant. The Sign was left behind."

"One accident: The brakes of a car failed. No evidence. Five people injured as collateral damage, two of whom may not make it."

"One long distance shooting with a stolen M25. The gun was left where it was fired from and the Sign was left next to it."

"The last one was shot with a Sig Sauer from close range. Left the gun in the target's hand together with the Sign", Diana explained.

By "the Sign" she meant the flower, Iris Chrysographes. It was her personal calling card, hence the nickname "Iris" or "Black Iris". No one had called her "Diana" for eleven years. Mainly because there was no one alive who knew it was her real name.

The boss examined the contents of the folders, paying extra attention to the photos and the written reports. They matched. Diana Sullivan had done it again. Sure she may act a bit arrogant towards him from time to time, but she got the job done better than anyone else.

Five targets in two weeks was an honourable achievement, considering all the targets had been in different countries at the time, and none of them had been what one would consider an easy one. It would take an average contract killer three times that long. He looked up at the woman and smiled.

"Good job, as always", he said, bent down behind the table, and lifted a briefcase on top of it.

"Ten million euros in cash, as agreed."

Diana opened the case without lifting it off of the table. She checked each bundle of notes individually to make sure no one was trying to trick them. Lastly, she took out a random note and checked for its authenticity. Pleased, she gave her boss a small nod. They hadn't been outfoxed this time.

"Not bad for a two weeks work. You have earned your break, Iris. Go and rest for a few days, but before that..." Nigel bent behind the desk and took out a folder, handed it to Diana, and continued:
"You can take this to take care of. I was a little sceptical at first, but the client insisted I send my best man on the job."

Diana took the folder and read the job description. She almost burst out laughing as she read it.

"A priest?" she looked at her boss in disbelief. "You want me to take care of a priest? Dear God, Nigel, I'm the one you'd send after President of the United States if it ever came up, and you want me to take care of a single priest?" Diana laughed.

These were going to be the easiest twenty million US dollars she had ever earned. To think someone was willing to pay that much for the life of one Protestant priest. Her normal pay was a couple hundred grand per job, but this month she'd had generous clients.

"I was thinking the exact same thing while listening to his requests, but he demanded that you'd be the one to take care of this", Nigel said while smiling. One didn't need to be a mind reader to know exactly what Iris was thinking.

"Who ordered the job?" Diana couldn't help but ask. The contract killer wasn't told the name of the client unless they asked for it. Unneeded information.

"The Universi", Nigel replied. It made sense. The Universi was an extreme atheist, extreme Darwinist secret society whose members shared the consensus that everything in the Universe was possible to explain using science.

It was natural for them to wish for this priest to die. Even Diana Sullivan had heard of him. The man had converted more people into Christianity than anyone else and he had more listeners than Billy Graham had had at his time. Some even claimed he had real spiritual powers.

As far as Miss Sullivan was concerned, all these claims were a load of crap. She did not believe in the existence of a God, or any deity for the matter, and looked at believers like there was something seriously wrong with them. How could anyone believe in something that could not be proven? Crazy, she thought.

Diana had seen a world most of us don't even want to imagine. Robberies, muggings, murders, rapes, and many other crimes too cruel to be described, as well as people ready to pay someone else to do all the dirty work for them. If the good God that priest was telling people about actually existed, it would not make any sense for him to allow all those things to happen.

Diana closed the folder and put it in her purse. They were allowed to express their opinion about the job they were given, but they still had to do it the way they were told by the client. This time the killing method was described as "Do whatever you want as long as he never brainwashes a single human ever again."

She'd observe her victim for a day and then take care of him in a way she saw most befitting. It was the Easter weekend, so she would break her habits and show up in a church on Friday.

Diana was just about to walk out the door as Nigel called out her name. She knew what was coming next. The boss did it to every one of his employees twice a year to make sure they could still be trusted. Diana turned to look at her boss.

"Yes?" she asked, knowing what was about to happen.

"If you were to ever get a job where the target was one of your colleagues or me, what would you do? After all, I'm the one who pays you", Nigel asked. A question many greenhorns who'd made it through the Final Test tripped over the first time they heard it.

Diana smiled with her vampire like grin, chuckled,

and answered the question:

"Pay me? Don't make me laugh. We both know very well that you don't pay me a single penny. My pay comes directly from the client's funds. "Employer" or "Boss" is just a title. In reality, you are just a messenger and a broker, and just as replaceable as the rest of us. Your successor has most likely been chosen already."

"And what comes to my colleagues, if any of them is careless enough to get a death warrant they deserve no mercy. In both cases, I'd do the job as instructed by the job description. Nothing personal, just business."

Diana meant every word she said. She had no feelings whatsoever for anyone she knew and she never allowed herself to get attached to anyone. Hard as a diamond, cold as liquid nitrogen. A perfect assassin.

The death warrant required a name, a photo (full face showing) and a likely location. If this information got out about an Organization assassin, they usually never made it past seven days after that. Diana however, wasn't worried about herself. She'd long time ago made sure her personal information could never get out.

Nigel was pleased at her answer and let her leave. *Good. Iris can still be trusted*', he thought. He dreaded the day his name would be inside a job folder as a target. It was, however, nearly impossible, for only those in the Organization knew what he looked like, and "Nigel Ramirez" wasn't even close to his real name.

Although it is to be noted that he himself only stepped into the boss' shoes three years ago exactly because the information about his predecessor had leaked. The killing method had been "A quarter kilo of C4 inside the drawer", and the person given the assignment had been no other than Diana Sullivan, Black Iris.

The bomb went off as the unlucky gentleman opened the drawer of his desk for the last time. What a mess... The newbies were repairing the office for a week and what had been left of the body had not been a pretty sight.

The fear was justified. Black Iris had no feelings, affections, or relationships that could hinder the job, and she made no mistakes. She always succeeded. Or at least that's what Nigel, other assassins and contract killers, mafia, Interpol, Iris herself, and all those who knew about her believed.

No one could have guessed that this easy mission was going to be the last one Iris ever did, and the reason for that is most likely not what you readers think.

Chapter 2.

Good Friday. The day when 2000 years ago a man they called Christ was crucified. There's just no limit to how despicable creatures those humans could be. Celebrating a day when people sentenced to death a man who presumably did nothing wrong in his entire lifetime.

Again another reason for Diana to consider Christians completely insane. Today however, she was one of them. She sat in a church among believers, listening a sermon spoken by a person she was supposed to kill ASAP.

Diana wasn't concerned about getting caught. She was one of world's best actors and a master of disguise. Hollywood actors would be green with envy if they knew.

She had covered the redness of her eyebrows with waterproof mascara and hidden her short red hair with a long reddish brown real hair wig. The unusual colour of her eyes was masked with green contact lenses. Just a thin silicone mask to alter facial features and a natural looking makeup and she was ready to go. Even if there were living witnesses (which was astronomically unlikely), they could never pick her out from a lineup.

From an outside observer's point of view, that particular assassin didn't stick out at church any more than any other woman did. She didn't look suspicious and behaved in a way the situation demanded, while at the same time keeping a keen eye on her target, observing his every move. The smallest details could be crucial in determining the killing method.

The job description required her to leave the Sign, so the method could be as flashy as she wanted, but that wasn't her style. She preferred more indirect methods such as accidents or poisons.

Staging an accident would prove to be difficult in this case, because the priest didn't have a car and practically lived in the church. She didn't see anything around her that could be used for that purpose. She decided to investigate the place more thoroughly at night.

During the sermon, Diana recited in her head the unwritten basics of the Organization's work instructions as she listened to the sermon just enough to be able to pretend she was paying attention the whole time.

***

The contract killers and assassins of the Organization have many rules and following them can be anything between important and essential to succeed on a mission. At times one could ignore some of the basics, but at most times it paid to follow them all, and the first three should never be neglected.

The instructions were something like the Ten Commandments of the Organization:

1. Never reveal your true identity to anyone.
2. Never become a visible piece of the puzzle you're creating.
3. Don't leave behind evidence of yourself that could lead to an arrest.
4. Do not contact the target if you can avoid it.
5. Wear a disguise outside the Base.
6. Follow the instructions in the work description.

7. Complete the mission as quickly as possible.
8. Do not let the target know they're being watched.
9. Learn to know the target's routines and/or environment.
10. Don't leave any witnesses.

The order of importance varied based on the job description and quality of the mission.

***

The event ended a bit too soon. Iris would have liked to observe her target for a bit longer, but leaving the church last was not an option. These three hours would have to do. Now she'd just return to her hotel, make a plan, and the next day...

Something stopped her mid thought. She didn't know what it was, but somehow she was unable to move. She turned to look at her target. He was having a conversation with a mother of two as the kids, possibly twins, were holding her hand tightly and hanging there, looking bored.

The mother thanked the man for an enlightening sermon and left the church with her kids, escorted by her husband. Diana was now alone in the church with her target.

The priest looked at Diana and had she not known better, she could have sworn he was looking right into her soul.

She turned to leave but before she had time to take a single step,

"Young lady, please stay for a moment", the priest said.

Diana wanted to run out of that building as fast as she could. Something about the atmosphere just didn't feel right. But the assassin knew how suspicious it would look if she were to hurry out. She smiled a weak smile and broke rule number four.

"Yes Father, did you wish to talk about something?" she asked.

At that moment something unexpected happened. Something no living soul could have known to expect. No one, including Diana, ever considered this day would come.

"You can stop acting, miss Diana Sullivan. I know why you're here", the priest said. Diana felt like she had been placed in the line of fire of her own shotgun. She hadn't been called by that name by anyone in a long time.

How did that man know her name? It was, of course, possible that against all expectations he had been tipped off and they were under surveillance this very moment. The best course of action would be to continue acting and play dumb.

"Who? I'm sorry but you must be mistaking me for someone else. My name is Sarah Evans and I came here to hear your sermon. You're just as convincing as they say you are", Diana said while smiling, perfectly acting.

Sarah Evans was one of her aliases and she had a real fake passport (real passport, fake information) in her bag. The priest, for some reason, could not be fooled.

"No need to worry. No human is observing us in any way. You must be wondering how I know who you are.

You probably wouldn't believe me even if I told you", the priest said to her. Diana asked the man to tell anyway and he did:

"I had a vision about you last night. The Lord told me to prepare for my time was up. This was my last sermon and I know it." The man had been right. Diana did not believe a word he said about a 'vision' or 'words of God' but for some reason, the man was right about this having been his last sermon. He also knew something not even the leader of the Organization knew: Diana's name.

She decided not to take chances. She reached into her purse and took out a NAA22S pocket pistol equipped with a silencer, and aimed the barrel at the priest.

"In that case you know it's no use running. One way or another you are going to get a .22 calibre bullet or two into your skull so do yourself a favour and let it be over quickly", Diana said without any sigh of empathy.

The priest fell on his knees, put his hands together and looked up at the ceiling. Diana chuckled. Great. Was the priest planning on begging for his life now? What came out of his mouth was not what Diana expected:

"Lord, have mercy on her. She doesn't know you and doesn't understand what she's doing. Open her eyes. Do what ever it takes and save that soul." The smile disappeared from Diana's face. She pressed the gun against the priest's temple, and he didn't resist.

"There's no such thing as God", she said in a cold voice and pulled the trigger.

***

Diana could not sleep that night. It had nothing to do with remorse for she never grieved her victims. Something just was not normal. Diana went through today's events. Things had gone completely unexpectedly.

How the hell was she supposed to explain this to her boss without mentioning that the priest had known both her identity and her purpose for being in the church? She'd have to lie in her report for the first time in her entire life and she'd have to be pretty damn good at it. If the written report didn't match crime scene photos there would be a resting place waiting for her six feet under.

The report laid unfinished on a desk with pictures spread all over the worktop. What kind of explanation would work with these photos without revealing the biggest screw up of the entire career of Black Iris? Sure she'd completed the mission. The man would never speak again, but he had known things he should never have known. Explaining that would be more difficult than writing a convincing report.

In three hours, the report was finished. It was straight forward and believable, and it was fundamentally similar to her former reports. Nigel would not be able to tell the difference between her real report and this partially made up one. Now there was only one mystery left to solve.

The young woman didn't want to include the supernatural in her theories as she was desperately trying to come up with an explanation to how the priest had found out her name.

No matter how hard she tried, she couldn't come up with a logical explanation. Diana Sullivan was officially dead. Drowned in a boating accident with her mother as a storm rose without a warning. The body was, of course, never found.

To this day, Diana remembered it like yesterday. The day she killed her own mother as part of her training and at the same time, faked her own death.

From her mother, she'd inherited her hair and her job, and she hadn't mourned for long. Killing the next of kin was what was considered "the final test" in the Organization.

By tradition, the Organization contract killers raise their children into the profession. Teach them all they need to know to do their job properly and at the end of the training, tell their child to kill them just to root out all unnecessary emotion left.

Those who did not obey the order within five minutes of hearing it, paid the ultimate price for their hesitation. Diana herself hadn't hesitated for an instant before pushing her mother overboard, letting the random storm raging over the area take care of the rest. Afterwards she had sailed to shore far from the harbour and let the waves take the boat away.

The broken yacht was discovered the next day and the body of a woman a week later. The officials searched for Diana for three months with no result and eventually, declared her dead without a body.

**

Diana put her report into her bag so she wouldn't forget it later, finished her cup of coffee and looked at the clock. Four in the morning. She'd been up all night. The redhead had tried to get some sleep on multiple occasions with no avail. He priests words wouldn't leave her alone.

'Great. I'm being haunted by a priest's ghost', Diana thought with a small smile on her lips. She made a decision to go to work early today. No use sitting around in a hotel if she wasn't going to sleep anyway.

Diana took her bag and was ready to leave as she suddenly dropped it from her hands and fell on her knees. She rubbed her eyes and looked in front of her again. She was either asleep or had officially gone crackers.

What was standing in front of her was a man dressed in white. He looked strong despite having a delicate frame and his back was decorated with large pure white wings.

God's angel. The thought sounded absurd. However, Diana would have noticed had anyone walked into her room uninvited, but none of the traps she'd set had gone off. The creature in front of her was either not human or was better with traps than Diana herself.

Diana shook her head violently. She must have dozed off at some point. She didn't think she'd lost her mind but then again, most patients committed in mental institutions don't think of themselves as crazy. The woman pulled herself together, stood up and smiled wryly.

"This is the strangest dream I have ever had", she said to the angel standing in front of her. A smile rose onto the angel's face that did not quite fit its innocent looks. The next moment Diana was lying on her side on the floor, her cheek stung and her ears were ringing. It took a while for her to understand that she had been hit. Hard.

"Sorry to tell you, but this is no dream", the angel said, still wearing that same smile. "I'm here and as you can tell, I'm real."

Diana stood back up, placing her hand on her sore cheek. She didn't want to believe what she saw but she didn't have a choice. Had all this been a dream she would have woken up the moment she was struck, and the angel would have disappeared into thin air.

That's not what happened. The angel was standing exactly where he'd been three seconds ago. She glared at the angel with an ice cold gaze. Never in her life had she ever been this annoyed.

"Who are you?" she asked.

"Michael", the angel answered, "You may have heard of me. I'm one of the archangels and lead the army of Heaven. Although, today I'm on a totally different job." The angel who'd just introduced himself as Michael sighed. Why did *he* have to be given this assignment? Usually if similar missions were given to archangels, they were given to Gabriel or Rafael. What *did* that priest see in this woman?

"An archangel?" Diana smiled sarcastically, "For an angel you are pretty violent. Don't know how you got in but you have to do better than that if you want me to believe a whacking lie like that." She pulled out of her sleeve a knife she'd concealed there and threw it, aiming at the middle of Michael's chest.

A bulls-eye wasn't celebrated for long. The blade flew right through the man and imbedded itself in the wall behind him. Diana was dumbstruck. She felt dizzy and for a moment she was sure she'd faint. The angel had hit her so he was obviously a solid creature. However, the knife had flown right through him without any resistance and without doing any damage.

'Hallucination?' she thought. She had read from somewhere that hallucinations could feel very real to the people experiencing them, without there being anything real about them.

She'd definitely neglected sleep for way too long... She'd accept her boss's vacation offer immediately after reporting her last job, and demand a vacation if he'd changed his mind for one reason or another.

Diana picked up her bag and recovered her knife, hiding it back into her sleeve, no longer paying any sort of attention to the angel. She removed all the traps and left. Michael didn't like being ignored.

Stubborn redhead... If things carried on the way they were that woman would burn in hell after her demise, which of course was not par of the Almighty's plan. Be Diana a killer or not, Michael had to find a way to break that heart, hardened from the moment of birth.

But the woman thought he was nothing more than a hallucination. How could one even proceed from that kind of situation? Or wait a minute... Perhaps he could use it to his advantage.

Chapter 3.

A phone rang. There would have been nothing special about it had it not been the classified number of a Canadian Interpol agent, Iovis Sterling. That phone ringing could mean only one thing: Black Iris had struck again.

The man had served as a liaison between countries in relation to that serial killer for five years now. It was a record, for Black Iris was like ICPO's hot potato. No agent assigned to the case worked on it for long. Before Iovis joined the investigation, nearly ten different agents had worked on the case of the Iris.

Iovis answered the phone, not surprised to hear the news. There had been a murder in Southampton, England, that was possibly related to Black Iris. The crime scene investigation had only just begun and there was no way to say for sure if it was the famous serial killer or a copycat, but Iovis was being asked to arrive at the scene nonetheless. His information about Black Iris could speed up the investigation so police wouldn't need to waste time chasing the wrong culprit.

Iovis ended the call and packed his bags. He'd hoped to soon get back home to Toronto to his wife and ten-year-old son, but it looked like his visit to Europe would continue for a while longer.

The man sighed deeply. Why did he spend time chasing that criminal who hadn't been caught yet despite all the time they'd had? Among law enforcement, Black Iris held another nickname: The Ghost. Nearly ten years had passed since the first confirmed murder and the only piece of physical evidence they had, was the flower left at the crime scenes. Frustrating...

Iovis grabbed his phone once again and booked himself a ticket to the first bus from London to Southampton he'd make it to. The killer must not escape from him this time! He could only rush to the crime scene and hope Iris had finally made a mistake. He needed just a bit more evidence related to the killer's identity. Just one more clue he had no idea he was carrying in his wallet. Just one more...

***

The half lie had passed unchallenged. Nigel had read the report and accepted it as the truth. No one would ever know what truly happened at the church.

Diana had demanded a vacation claiming migraine, and her boss had believed her. She'd be assigned her next job after a month. Removing a source of stress, however, had not changed one fact: Michael was still there. What exactly was it going to take to get rid of the angel?

Sure, Diana wanted to visit a doctor, but finding a suitable person would not be easy. Due to her profession, public healthcare was out of the question and there weren't many underground doctors around.

"Do you plan on hovering around for long?" Diana asked for no particular reason.

"Until my work is done and it looks like it's going to take a while", Michael answered while poking a mirror that did not show his reflection. There was nothing strange about the reflection not showing for Michael wasn't in a full corporeal form. His reflection could not be seen from any reflective surface. Diana was the only one who could see him. Boring, but orders were orders... The last thing needed was mass panic.

"If your job is to convert me, don't waste your time and get lost! You're not even real. Just an illusion! Why the hell should I be paying any attention to a word you say?" The angel's attitude was really pissing Diana off. Michael smiled wryly and said:

"Just an illusion eh? Listen to yourself. If you're right, then you're hallucinating about someone you have never seen, whom you've barely heard about and before all, in whose existence you don't even believe in. Human brain is an interesting thing is it not?"

Michael was right... Diana had never seen that face and couldn't remember hearing about archangel Michael. She was a professional killer for crying out loud! She'd never gone to school and her mother had mostly taught her about things necessary for profession. Religion was not part of it. What she knew about religion she'd found out through media or heard from passers by.

"Leave it!" she snapped at Michael and headed to the door. She needed fresh air. In a seaside city like Southampton that may actually be possible.

***

People often say they'd believe in God if he'd only show himself to them. Diana was living proof that this way of thinking was false. She did not believe in deities or angels, and Michael's presence hadn't changed that one bit.

Walking through the alleys of Southampton with an angel at her side whom only she could see, Iris still believed it to be nothing more than a hallucination caused by stress and lack of sleep. It was the only option she was willing to accept.

It's no use saying others wouldn't do the same. Humans are stubborn creatures who, when convinced about one reality will not even consider other alternatives even if one were to jump at them from underground and bite their bottom. The world would be a different kind of place if they could.

Diana had no clear destination. She just walked around while at the same time observing her environment, trying not to think about what had happened the day before. She never would have thought this unplanned route would take her back to that church. It felt disturbingly like someone was out to get her.

***

"A church should not feel this grim..." Iovis sighed. He was standing in front of the altar where the murdered man's body had lain the moment it was found. Iovis had seen plenty of photos but what set him apart from other Interpol agents was his desire to always see the crime scene with his own eyes and to actively participate in the investigation. Black Iris was like his nemesis and photographs weren't nearly enough for him.

The murderer had to have visited the scene during yesterday's gathering, but as always, churches didn't keep a list of people coming and going. There wasn't even a register people could sign... The crime scene was a dead end just like all the previous ones had been.

Iovis told the crime scene investigator he'd seen enough, and left the church only to stop like hitting a wall. On the other side of the police tape a young woman was approaching the church. He couldn't say why or how, but there was something awfully familiar about her.

The girl was tall, about 175 cm (about 5'9"), slim but fit. She had deep red hair and chestnut eyes. However, something about her didn't feel real. Like she was a ghost.

The man woke up from his trance and walked up to the woman.

"This is a crime scene. The church will be closed for a while", he said to the woman. That woman was Diana. She stopped next to the police tape, looked him in the eyes and smiled, looking like she had nothing to do with the bloody act that had taken place in that church.

"I wasn't going to the church. I just saw the police tape from the other side of the street and got curious. What happened in here?" Diana asked, faking confusion.

She knew she'd have to watch her words. The albino man wasn't wearing a uniform but him being on the other side of the police tape without the cops making a deal out of it proved that he worked for some other law organization. Most likely Interpol.

Iovis knew neither what to think of the woman nor what to say to her. Technically one weren't allowed to discuss an active investigation but unlike a year ago, Black Iris was no longer a state secret and this particular case had already leaked it's way to the media in the form of extra news. It would be in the papers tomorrow. Just where did those damn reporters get their information from anyway?

One way or another, this case was more or less public information and so the man decided it wouldn't hurt to give a shallow answer. Who knows, the general public might turn out to be helpful and in this situation and he needed all the help he could get.

"Black Iris happened. That serial killer struck again", Iovis said to the woman. Diana reacted appropriately: With shock spiced with fear.

On the inside however, she felt lucky. If she'd play her cards right she could potentially send the police and governments on a wild goose chase so bad they'd have no choice but to drop the investigations. Alternatively, she could throw the blame on any person or group she wanted.

"Black Iris? The serial killer that's been chased for years? You still haven't caught him? No way he hasn't left behind any evidence after all these murders", Diana was almost yelling at the agent. For her, respecting elders was too much to ask, not to mention any civilian would have reacted the same.

Iovis felt embarrassed. She had a point. After all these years, Iris should have already been caught.

"I'm really sorry. We're doing everything we can but Iris is a lot more skilled than believed at first. Usually a serial killer reveals more and more about himself with every murder but the more Black Iris kills, the more he seems to deceive us", the man managed to answer her. As soon as he'd said it, he placed his hand at his mouth and said:

"I'm sorry. I've spoken too much. Shouldn't have said that." The agent was feeling uncomfortable but Diana was overjoyed. They had nothing and she had succeeded at her job.

At that exact moment Michael thought it best to tap the woman's shoulder twice with his index finger. Diana flinched and looked over her shoulder. She'd totally forgotten about the angel.

"Doesn't matter if you think of me as real or not. I can still work as your voice of conscience. Now would be a good time to do the right thing", Michael said to her. Diana didn't let it show on the outside and simply pretended to swat a bug sitting on her shoulder thinking. *'Shut up! Are you suggesting I should give myself in!? Dream on!'*

Iovis paid no attention to the gesture. People flinch for the strangest reasons and bugs were among them. He hadn't seen an insect, but right now he wouldn't notice one buzzing right in front of his nose. He was too focused on wondering why that woman looked so familiar.

Iovis didn't know he was staring, but Diana picked up on it in no time.

"Why are you staring at me? Is there something on my face?" she asked him directly. Diana knew the albino had no way of knowing she was the killer, but the stare still made her feel uncomfortable. Iovis realized what he was doing and looked away immediately.

"Sorry. Didn't mean to stare... It's just that... You seem familiar somehow. Have we met somewhere before?" Iovis asked. Diana shook her head and said she'd never seen him before. Iovis apologized one more time and Diana turned to leave.

At that moment the albino was struck with a thought. It sounded impossible, but he chose to ask about it anyway. He asked the woman to wait. Diana stopped, turned around and asked with her gaze what it was the man wanted now.

"This may sound strange but... Do you happen to know anyone called Juno Sullivan?" Iovis asked.

Deadly silence. Diana almost lost her cool. How did he know? How the hell did that man know the name of Diana's mother!? Diana pulled herself together, took a deep breath and answered: "No. Who is she?"

Iovis took out his wallet and picked out a photograph he then showed Diana.

"She's a woman I knew over twenty years ago. She disappeared into thin air and I haven't seen her since. To me you look a lot like her", Iovis explained. Diana said she failed to see the resemblance. She didn't know how that man knew her mother but it did not matter as long as the agent didn't find out the relationship between Diana and Juno.

Diana found it best to leave the scene as fast as possible. The man had unknowingly struck Diana right in her Achilles heel and there was no way she could let him take advantage of it. She said goodbye to the agent who, just in case, gave her his calling card.

Diana had no intention to call and reveal information but she took the card as a courtesy, and to get his name. If things turned south, she could get rid of him at any time. Diana looked at the card and read the name and organization written on it: Iovis Sterling,

Interpol.

***

As soon as she'd gotten far away from the crowd, Diana stopped and looked at Michael.

"How did he know?" she asked not bothering to be more specific. No matter how you look at it, she was not in a good mood. Diana hadn't heard her mother's name uttered since the day she died.

Michael didn't look like he'd heard the question. The angel was looking at the sky and appeared to be in a world of his own. He'd known the Lord had something in mind for the good of Diana, but bringing THAT man into the picture was unexpected. What good would that be? The man didn't even know he had a d...

Diana had enough of being ignored and punched Michael in the head. Sure she couldn't harm the angel, but anyone would snap out of it if they saw someones fist coming out of their face.

"Did you not hear me? How did that man know Juno!?" Diana was shouting. It was fortunate there were no people around to see or hear, because it would have looked like Diana was talking to herself.

Michael rubbed his forehead. He hadn't felt any pain but still, what that human being had just done had not felt nice. Should he just tell her what she wanted to know? There was no harm in it. Maybe...

"Iovis wasn't the target, but he was involved in an assignment your mother screwed up in more ways than one. I'm not saying more", Michael explained. Diana tried to punch Michael again. She couldn't stand it when someone referred to Juno as her mother. Not after what Diana had had to go through because of her.

It didn't take long for rage to turn to wonder. Juno screwed up an assignment? Impossible. It wasn't public knowledge, but Juno was the best of her time. Her calling card had been the ace of spades, but it was left extremely seldom, for her speciality were unsolved assassinations and setups. Juno was responsible, for example, for the assassination of a weapons engineer whose killer is still being searched for in the wrong place. Her reign had, however, been short lived when... Hold on... No, no, no... It couldn't be!

Diana fell on her knees. She could not believe the conclusion she'd just come to. There were over seven billion people in the world, half of whom were men, and if Diana was right, Iovis Sterling wasn't just another stranger. The coincidence felt almost like a cliche.

Diana pulled herself together, standing up once again. This changed nothing. Momentary shock had been wiped away and Black Iris was her normal self once again: An emotionless killing machine. Michael was once again just a voice between her ears and meeting Iovis was just a mindless coincidence.

"This is stupid... Juno is dead and should be forgotten", Diana sighed. Michael couldn't help but smile as he said:

"And despite that she still has an effect on your life. That's what you humans are like. The dead can't be forgotten until there's no one left alive who could possibly remember them, and they influence your lives whether you want it or not."

"Juno mistreated you so you wish to forget about her but you can't, because whether you want it or not, she was and will always be the woman who brought you into this world knowing it would kill her."

Didn't that angel know when to shut up!? A person familiar with the bible would be able to tell you that on its pages Michael doesn't have many lines to say. In the real world, however, it seemed like he was in love with the sound of his own voice, and to make things worse, whenever he spoke he always hit the nail on the head.

Diana felt a sting in her heart. Michael felt more and more real every moment and she had to constantly remind herself that he wasn't. She also knew what the angel was going at and she didn't hesitate to point it out:

"Once again, you're trying to convince me that God exists. You are wasting your time."

"You're half right. My mission is to guide you so you could accept the existence of God and accept Christ's sacrifice. Long story short, my mission's not over before you are either no longer on your way to Hell or dead. Whichever comes first", Michael corrected. It didn't take two seconds before Diana said that there was neither Heaven nor Hell.

Michael sighed deeply. He felt sorry for that woman. If it were easy, there would be no need for an angel, but under normal circumstances Diana wouldn't meet anyone who could help her. She required time and most people didn't have enough of it to give. Michael moved close to the woman and gently hugged her.

"Diana... Why can't you believe in Him?" Michael

asked with sadness in his voice. Diana found the situation unfair. Why could she feel the angel's touch when he allowed it but not touch him herself at any other time? She wanted to pull away from the grip but couldn't, so she decided to answer the angel's crazy sounding question:

"How could I? How could I believe in God when I live in this God forsaken world where there's need for someone like me? You're a figment of my imagination so you know very well what I've seen and experienced. If God is good, shouldn't the world be? But it isn't. The world is rotten to the core. Even if there is a God, it's not the God you're talking about."

Michael let go of her and looked up at the sky, like he was expecting to hear speech from that direction. What happened next was so ridiculous the only reason it was put in this book was because it was meaningful for the plot...

Michael smiled. Then he chuckled and started laughing so hard there were tears flowing out of his eyes. It wasn't the evil or mean kind of laughter. More like he'd just heard something amusing.

"You're angry at him, aren't you?" the angel managed to say through the laughter. Diana had no idea how she should react. This was the first time in her life anyone had ever laughed at her.

It took a while for Michael to pull himself back together. He still wore that amused expression on his face but at least he was no longer rolling in the aisles. The angel coughed and looked at Diana with pure sympathy in his eyes. He reached his hand out to her and said:

"There's something I want to show you. It's right around the corner." She didn't want to take that hand and she definitely did not want to go to where that figment of imagination wanted her to go. Still, she had nothing better to do and it couldn't hurt so she decided to swallow her pride this once. Diana lightly smacked Michael's hand saying she'd follow this once, but not holding hands.

Chapter 4.

"This is a church?" Diana asked looking at the three-storey building in front of her that had a cleaning company's office on the first floor, and on the second floor a psychiatric outpatient clinic was announcing it was moving to another address.

"In the "community" sense of the word. A church doesn't need an actual church building. It's enough that two or more people gather in His name. The place itself doesn't matter", Michael explained and walked right through the door, beckoning Diana to follow him, saying the door was unlocked. Reluctantly Diana grabbed the door handle and stepped inside.

Getting up those stairs was its own kind of challenge. After making it to the last step she for some reason she couldn't take it any more. On one hand she felt a strange desire to walk up that last step and step in through the glass doors, but on the other hand she could almost hear a voice telling her to turn back.

The silent demand had been ringing in her mind from the first step on and the higher she climbed the louder it became. By now the sound had become so loud she could almost hear it with her ears. Diana no longer knew which way to go.

Just as she was about to turn back she felt Michael placing his hands on her ears. At that moment the sound that had just a moment ago been ordering her to turn back quieted down. It wasn't gone completely but the hands of the archangel muffled it so well it might as well have gone silent.

"Don't listen to the Devil's whispers. Instead of making him happy, how about doing what *you* want to do?" the angel said quietly.

Diana thought about it for a moment. What *did* she want? Did she want to step through those glass doors or did she want to turn back? No... There was no turning back. When you've come this far, the only way to go is forward. Therefore, she took that last step and stepped through the glass doors into a place a minute ago she didn't know existed.

***

Diana felt slightly uncomfortable, walking in in the middle of a sermon. She was trying to keep a low profile, sitting down on a free chair at the very edge of the back-most row, but the young, barely 25-year-old, pastor holding the sermon made it clear in a silent gesture that he had noticed her arrival.

As the pastor kept on talking, Diana was being overcome by a suffocating feeling. No way she was getting back up though for Michael was keeping his hand on her shoulder. The angel couldn't make her believe, but the least he could do was to make sure she didn't take a hike right away.

The sermon ended and the church began to sing, and Diana was granted yet another surprise. She herself couldn't have been less interested in songs, especially Christian songs the lyrics to which she was unfamiliar with, but the person next to her was singing like an angel. Literally...

Diana wouldn't have believed it had she not heard it herself. Michael's singing voice was one of the most beautiful ones she'd ever heard. Soft yet strong and full of emotion. As an angel, Michael couldn't fully relate to the lyrics written by humans but the praise that could be heard in his voice was still at least as strong as that of all the people present.

Before the last song had fully ended, Diana brushed Michael's hand off her shoulder and turned to leave. She hadn't managed to get past the glass doors as she heard the young pastor behind her saying:

"Are you leaving already? The service may be over but coffee and conversations are just beginning. Why not stay for a while? First timers don't need to pay in the cafeteria."

Diana was about to refuse, but decided to stay anyway. It couldn't hurt and in her situation, free coffee sounded extremely good.

Diana was still feeling uncomfortable as she sat around the table with the pastor. On top of that, Michael had become strangely silent, which was not helping. He just stood there, leaning against the windowsill and observing the situation, not saying a word. Still, Diana was the only one who could see the angel and so only she felt his observing gaze in the back of her neck.

"Why can't you believe in Him?"

Michael's question was echoing in her mind. Diana thought of God's existence as something impossible and yet for some reason the figment of her own imagination was doubting her world view. It made no sense.

Diana glanced at the coffee sipping pastor and decided to ask a question that had been plaguing her mind for many, many years:

"How can you just blindly believe in something that can't be proven?" The pastor didn't seem to be the least bit bothered by the question, like he'd heard it a million times before.

"If something could be proven unequivocally, it would no longer be a question of 'faith' but 'knowledge'. Many believe blindly in the Theory of Evolution or the Big Bang Theory which are taught to people as facts but are by the definition of science just as unreliable as almost any religion."

"However, Christianity has on it's side the recorded historic evidence found in the Bible which has been proven reliable, so the claim that there would be no proof at all is by any means false."

"But faith is not based on solid evidence for even if God were to show himself to humans personally it would not force them to believe. Christ lived among people and they still did not believe in him", he answered. It was a convincing reply, at least in Diana's opinion. This was at that a good moment for a follow-up question:

"What makes you think the Bible is reliable?"

Once again, the pastor wasn't bothered. He explained that going through all the facts would, however, take all night, and mentioned a certain Oxford University literary professor had once studied the Bible thoroughly as a book and come to a conclusion that it could only be one of two things: Either exactly what it claims to be or the best hoax in the entire history of mankind.

Faking something like the Bible out of nothing would have been impossible under the circumstances. The pastor mentioned the name of the book that dealt with the issue as well as a few other works that processed the reliability of the Bible. He even offered to lend the works he owned, but Diana politely declined. She'd made it a habit to not borrow anything she couldn't return with certainty.

It looked like Christianity wasn't totally baseless. As the conversation moved on it piqued Diana's curiosity and she asked the pastor if he had a more personal reason for believing in God if faith had nothing to do with evidence.

"Just as I'd turned eighteen I happened to be at the wrong place at the wrong time. I ended in a crossfire and was hit by several bullets. I was rushed to a hospital as fast as possible. During the operation my heart stopped several times and I spent three weeks in a coma. I wasn't supposed to make it, but here I am. It wasn't hard for my sister to get me into church after that and soon I ended up as a pastor", he explained.

"How can you be so sure it wasn't just about the skill of the doctors and a lot of good luck?" Diana couldn't help but ask.

"Do you know what 'the aorta' is?" he asked. Of course she knew, and could even point out it's location while the heart is still hidden inside the body.

The aorta is the main artery of the human body, originating from the heart. If it bursts, it is nearly always fatal due to the heavy bleeding, which made it a good place to aim with a gun when going for a certain death but the head was impossible to hit.

Diana was in disbelief as she found out one of the bullets had ruptured the priest's aorta, and he was still alive. For a moment Diana doubted the truthfulness of the story, but the pastor was willing to prove it to be true no matter what he had to do.

Diana continued her conversation with the pastor, asking many faith related questions. This was the first time ever Diana had had the opportunity to have this sort of conversation with anyone. She was rather surprised as the pastor answered her every question with confidence, convincingly justifying his answers as if he were in an actual debate. The pastor spoke as if he knew exactly how to deal with the redhead sitting in front of him.

As the conversation carried on, Diana wondered why she hadn't left before it started. Was it because Michael had told her not to listen to the Devil's whispers? Did she somewhere inside her truly want to hear what that young man had to say?

She didn't know anymore. The only thing at that moment that was for certain was that Diana's world view was falling apart at the seams, bit by bit. By the minute, it became more and more difficult to deny God's existence.

"You know... What I find the most intriguing is that those who don't believe in God always first adduce that there is no evidence, when the absence of evidence is not the evidence of absence."

"It's considerably more easy to prove that something exists than that something doesn't. In theory, a sufficient proof of existence is to find the object in question. Whereas in the absence of solid evidence it is impossible to prove that something doesn't exist, for there is always the possibility it just hasn't been found", the pastor said, finishing his cup of coffee.

In theory? Diana was about to ask as she remembered what the pastor had said earlier. People don't always believe even in what they see.

She glanced once again at the angel standing by the window, at present killing time around his fingernails. Earlier he'd been eavesdropping on conversations at the table next to theirs, but the masses had already scattered and Diana and the pastor were the only ones there.

At that time, the topic of their conversation switched from the existence of God to the Gospel, the life of Jesus and salvation. Diana was listening to the pastor, perhaps a bit curious. She hadn't heard about the subject before in such clarity and detail.

***

"I can't become a Christian", Diana said quietly. Michael was looking at hear direction as if saying "we'll see about that", and the pastor just smiled and said:

"No one is going to force you to decide right away. If you're not ready now, you can always accept salvation later, even on your deathbed. God's love knows no bounds. Anyone, absolutely anyone, no matter who they are or what they've done, can be saved at any time of their life and no matter what happens, you can't lose the gift of salvation."

Diana had heard enough about love. There were many things she didn't believe existed and love was one of them. The pastor was going to hear about it.

"God's love?" Diana asked, chuckled and continued: "There's no such thing as God... There's no love either... Where is love when a mother gives birth to a drug addicted baby and then abandons it just to get her next dose? Where was God when a child murdered her own parent with an axe? Where was god when a boy lusted after his sister and killed half the neighbourhood because of it, including her fiance? Where is God when people hire someone else to do the dirty work for them? Where is God... Where was God when my own mother raised me a killer!? Where's the love in that!?"

Diana was breathing heavily. At first talking to the pastor had been interesting but now she didn't want to hear another word from his mouth. She grabbed her bag and turned to leave only to see Michael standing in her way. In a manner different from before, he'd taken a full corporeal form so that the pastor too could see him.

In a powerful sounding voice, Michael told Diana to sit down. Diana was by no means happy about it but she obeyed saying:

"Are you going to preach about it too? I've said it before and I will say it again. There's no such thing as God and there's definitely no such thing as..."

"Love?" the angel finished her sentence, pressed both his hands against her shoulders and continued:

"How can you say there is no love when you yourself have experienced it in its greatest form? Think! It's true your upbringing left much to be desired but isn't your existence alone a proof of love!?"

Michael's voice was almost shaking. Just how lost could a human being be? Wasn't there anything that could help that lost lamb find it's way home? The angel was about to give up hope. He was ready to throw in the towel when he saw something in the woman's eyes no one had expected. It was a tear.

Chapter 5.

If a woman from the Organization got pregnant she had exactly three choices: Terminate the pregnancy, kill the child after birth or raise the child a killer. There was no fourth alternative. If the woman refused to raise her child into the profession and didn't kill it herself, someone from the Organization did it for her.

However, keeping the child often meant shortening their own lives. During the Final Test which the child would to at the age of 10-12, they'd have to kill their own mother. The women usually only kept the child at an older age whereas the younger ones, more often than not, chose to kill.

But Juno Sullivan had been only 17 years old when she found out she was expecting a child. She'd had her whole life ahead of her and it would have been crazy to cut it short before hitting the age of thirty. It would only have made sense for Diana to have died before she even got her name... But it didn't happen.

It took two decades for Diana to realize this. She'd lived the past fifteen years of her life hating her mother from the bottom of hear heart, but now Michael had changed that with only one sentence.

When people reject the truth, they build around themselves a protective barrier against it. The shield can be extremely strong, but one crack is enough to make it crumble into dust. Diana's shield had been cracked by the realization that her mother loved her. So much she'd give her life for her daughter.

Diana's world was in pieces. Everything she'd believed in and put her trust in every day had been torn apart in one single day. All the emotions she'd thought she'd gotten rid of erupted in one moment. Suddenly the faith and world view Christians had had become so real her old world view couldn't stand in front of it any longer.

After all the time spent with the angel and the conversation she'd had with the pastor she had to admit she had been wrong and they had been right. There is a Heaven, there is a Hell, there is a Devil and... and... There is a God.

Michael had barely let go of the woman as she already threw herself into his arms, buried her face into his shoulder and cried on it. Secretly she rejoiced in the fact that Michael was real because otherwise she'd be lying face down on the floor right now.

The gesture made the angel feel a bit awkward but Michael swallowed his pride and wrapped his arm around her.

"This was the first time you tried to touch me without the intent to kill", Michael said quietly.

At the same time Diana was being overcome by fear. She had acknowledged the truth but what did it help her? She would go to Hell anyway. There could be no salvation for a killer like her. During her life she'd denied God and killed hundreds of people, including at least one priest and Diana's own mother. The list of her sins was too long to be erased. Or so she thought.

Michael seemed to sense her fear and beckoned the pastor to come closer. The pastor obeyed, bowed slightly and said the meeting was an honour, and asked how he could help.

"Tell her what she needs to hear", Michael said

pointing at Diana with his free hand. The man knelt next to her, placed his hand on her shoulder, and spoke in a calm voice:

"Diana... As I told you already, God's love knows no bounds. No matter how severe your sins might be, they have already been paid for. Christ came down to Earth because no human is sinless enough to redeem themselves. He would have died for you had you been the only human in the world. And he didn't leave it there. He conquered the grave and rose from the dead, opening the gates to everlasting life to all who believe in Him. All you need to do is accept it. Just let God love you because, he already does."

Those words were hard to believe. It sounded insane that a heartless serial killer could be forgiven but... If it were possible after all... That's when Diana made up her mind that she'd take the leap of faith and accept what the angel spoke of and the pastor preached about. At that time she felt like she'd truly been saved.

Michael looked up and smiled in a way different from before. He hugged her tightly with both his arms before letting go and standing up.

"Well done. That was probably the best decision you've made in your life and definitely the most important one", the angel praised her and said: "This means that my work here is done. Time for me to return home."

Diana grabbed the angel by the sleeve and asked him not to leave. She felt she still needed Michael for she knew not what she should do. She'd been saved from Hell but life on earth wouldn't be easy from now on.

Michael touched her hand gently and said:

"You'll be fine without me. Just do what you see right. Besides, even if you can't actually see him, there's one of the best guardian angels standing beside you. And... You piqued my interest. I can guarantee you I'll be observing your life from Heaven and when your time on Earth is up, I promise I'll be there, escorting you home."

"Before you go... Could you answer one question?" Diana asked. Michael said he'd try.

"Why does evil exist? If God is good... Why would he create evil?"

Diana's question was a common one. Many, if not every believer had at some point of their lives wondered about the same thing.

"You can't assume you'll get all the answers on a silver plate. I wish I could answer that but it's a question you'll have to figure out the answer to yourself. Just keep this in mind: Although He may not directly cause everything, nothing happens unless He permits it for one reason or another", Michael explained with a sad smile.

The angel felt bad he couldn't give Diana a better answer. Diana didn't exactly like that vague answer but she accepted it. She'd understand one day. That was for sure.

Michael said goodby to Diana and the pastor, and stepped a few steps away from them. The area around him started shining so brightly the people in the room had to close their eyes or risk blindness. When Diana and the pastor finally opened their eyes, Michael had disappeared into thin air. Nonetheless, he had left a permanent mark in that young woman's heart and made an unforgettable memory of himself for two people.

Diana felt insecure. She knew what God wanted her to do and she wanted to do it but she didn't know how she'd pull it off. She stood up from the floor and sat on a chair. She looked up at the ceiling, placed her hands in her pockets and thought about it as she was fingering a piece of cardboard in her pocket.

A piece of cardboard? Diana took the card out of her pocket and looked at it. It was the calling card Iovis Sterling, the Interpol agent who'd known Juno, had given her. Of course! Why hadn't she thought of it right away!? She'd need a phone and a computer. She had a few disposable phones in her bag but...

"Do these church facilities have a computer I could use?" Diana asked the pastor who gave an affirmative answer.

One can lose nothing by believing in God,
yet gain everything by having faith in Him.
So why not believe?

Just because it can not be found
does not mean it can not exist.
But if it's found once,
no one can truly deny its existence.

Chapter 6.

Saturday had gone by fast and the investigation ha
gone nowhere. As usual, Black Iris hadn't left any
useful evidence behind. The church was a public
place, visited by hundreds of people each day, which
rendered any and all physical evidence worthless.

Didn't need to be a mind reader to know Iovis was
frustrated. When would this chase end? He was
constantly spending long time periods away from
home because of Iris. It had been a month since he'd
last seen his wife and son. Some would call it a
miracle Iovis was still into his first marriage and his
wife had never filed for divorce. The reason may be
that he took the time to call home every day.

At the very moment, Iovis was finishing a phone call
to his son. The boy was proud of his father and often
bragged about him at school, and was happy to listen
to all the stories Iovis was allowed tell. Before hanging
up, he said good night to his wife. It was still daytime
in Toronto, but in London it was already 10 pm.

Iovis was preparing to go to bed and was washing his
teeth as the phone rang. It was his public number so
the caller could have been pretty much anyone. He
spat out the toothpaste and flushed his mouth quickly
before answering the phone. Nothing in the world
could have prepared him for what he heard from the
other side of the line.

"This is Black Iris", the caller said. It was the voice of a
woman. Iovis almost dropped the phone. Black Iris
was calling him? Why on earth? There was always the
possibility it was a prank call but the Interpol agent
couldn't take the chance.

Iovis was about to use his other phone to call his colleague and ask them to trace the call as the caller suddenly stopped his intentions saying:

"Don't bother trying to trace this call. I'm not dumb enough to call from a traceable device when burner phones exist. Actually, don't even touch your second cell phone during this call or I'll make sure you'll regret it for the rest of your life."

"How do I know you really are Black Iris?" Iovis asked as he put down his other phone. The caller was prepared with an answer.

"I shot a priest in his own church right in the temple after all the other people in the church had left. I left my mark, a Black Iris, into his left hand, the stub of the stem between his index and ring finger. You visited the scene this morning", the caller explained.

Iovis hastily dug out the crime scene photo's. Everything matched, and more importantly, the details of this particular case had not been released to the media in that kind of detail. The caller had to be Black Iris, or at least the priest's killer.

"I'm listening", the man said and Iris spoke:

"Make sure to listen carefully because I'm not going to repeat anything. Prepare a pad and a pencil if you're not sure you can remember everything." Iris took a pause, as if giving him time to get the things for note taking (which he did) before continuing:

"I have no intention to discuss this on the phone. I want to talk face to face. When I end this call, reserve the first flight to Finland, Helsinki, you can make it to. The flight tomorrow morning should still have room.

You have the Interpol passport so the officials should let you into the country if you mention you're chasing an international serial killer."

"When you get to Helsinki, sign into any hotel of your choice in the city centre. Reserve a room today. I'll track you down and well meet there. Come alone. No colleagues, no reinforcements waiting inside or outside the hotel, no hidden cameras, no bugs."

Iovis was sceptical about the caller's intentions and didn't trust her as far as he could throw her. He knew this was most likely a trap and he had no intention to fall in it.

"What if I refuse?" Iovis asked.

"You have a beautiful wife and a cute son. If you refuse, I can't guarantee their safety", the caller answered. The sentence caused a chill to run down the man's spine.

"You wouldn't dare!!!" Iovis was shouting into the phone. He could take it when someone threatened his life, but threatening his family was going too far.

"Try it and see. The same warning also applies to not obeying all the instructions right down to the letter. Obey and nothing happens to them."

"Also, I have no intention to kill you, but if you're having doubts about it, you may be armed. Just keep in mind that for the fairness' sake, so am I", Iris answered calmly. Iovis had no choice but to agree to her demands. He feared for his life but the safety of his family was more important.

The call ended and Iovis fell down on his bed. He spent a moment staring at the ceiling thinking about what had just happened before getting up, starting the computer in his hotel room and doing as he'd been told.

***

If the citizens of Helsinki knew who the man who'd just signed into a hotel had come to meet, the whole city would be in panic. However, the citizens were living their lives, each celebrating Easter in their own way, ignorant of what was going on behind the curtain.

This wasn't the first time Iovis came to Finland. Iris had killed here too. About a year earlier a visiting politician had met his end at Ring Road III due to the breaks failing, and the under the hood there had been the symbol of Black Iris. Back then the visit had been just business. Now his visit was part job, part personal.

Iovis opened the door to his room and was about to take off his shoes as he froze in his place In the room's shoe rack there was a neatly placed pair of woman's shoes and a black windbreaker was hanging from the stand. Iovis put down his suitcase, took out his gun, assembled it, loaded it and carefully stepped into the room,

"Took you long enough. I was beginning to worry", a young woman laying on the couch said as she saw him. She had blood red hair and amethyst coloured eyes. She was slim and fit and definitely the same woman Iovis had met the day before, in front of the church.

Iovis mentioned the flight being delayed as he slowly moved towards the woman. She was wearing skin tight clothes she couldn't conceal a handkerchief in, never mind a gun. This caused him to relax just a bit, even though he didn't put his weapon down.

"Are you Black Iris?" he asked her. She sat up, nodded and patted the sofa with her hand saying:

"Do sit down. I won't bite." Iovis replied that he preferred to stand. Sitting next to the woman would put him at her mercy.

"I have no doubt about your responsibility for what happened on Friday, but are you really Black Iris? You do know who you're claiming to be, right?" Iovis asked to make sure he was dealing with the right person. There was no physical evidence so a confession would mean everything, and Iovis did not want to convict the wrong person.

The most suspicious thing about this confession was the woman's age. If she was who she claimed to be, she would've had to have been a young girl when she started killing.

She'd been expecting the question. She leaned forward and went through ten newest Black Iris murders in great detail.

"Do you want me to continue?" she asked as she'd finished. Iovis said he'd heard enough to be convinced of her identity as the wanted serial killer. There was only one thing left he needed to be answered.

"What do you want?" Iovis asked.

Iris adjusted her posture, looked him directly in the eyes and said:

"I want to stop killing." Iovis couldn't believe his ears. Her next request however was very much predictable and he didn't let her say it.

"Let me guess. You want me to help you with it? No chance. You went too far when you threatened my family. I should shoot you here and now", Iovis said, meaning every word.

"Your wife and son were never in danger. It was an empty threat, meant only to get your attention. Didn't believe you'd have come here otherwise", the Iris pointed out gesturing the man to put down his gun.

She'd taken the risk this would happen and that's exactly why she'd come unarmed. Were she carrying a gun, or even a knife, the Interpol agent standing in front of her would not hesitate to carry out his threat.

Iovis lowered his gun, understanding the woman was right. Nonetheless, he had no will to help this woman. He couldn't even comprehend why Black Iris was asking for help. Especially from him.

"You must be wondering why I'm asking for help when I might as well just disappear", Iris pointed out. Iovis nodded and she continued:

"The answer lies in why I kill at all. I'm a contract killer and working for a larger organization. One of the rules is that no one leaves the business other than to the grave. If I just quit, my replacement will hunt me down and do his job." As she said the last sentence, Diana made a gesture with her fingers, like she was shooting herself in the head.

Iovis understood now why Iris was asking for help but one thing was still unclear.

"Why me? How do you think I can, or why I'd even want to help you?" he asked. Diana sighed and explained:

"I didn't know who else to turn to. Whether you want it or not, you've been chasing me longer than anyone else and so you know me the best."

"There's also the fact that you work for Interpol that can help. You can help arrange an international meeting that I may use to get a deal that benefits me."

"Don't get me wrong. I'm not trying to be pardoned. I just want to be convicted in Finland according to Finland's laws. That way I may one day see the world outside the bars again and start being useful to society. In return I'll give an official confession and tell you everything you want to know about the Organization and about my clients."

Diana stood up and walked to him. She quickly grabbed Iovis' wallet from his pocket and backed away back to the couch saying:

"As for your willingness to help, the answer can be found in here." Before Iovis could demand a more specific answer, Diana took out the photo of her mother and held it next to her face so that the man could compare them.

"When I denied knowing her I lied. The truth is that Juno...", Diana took a deep breath and admitted something she hadn't said in years, followed by something that almost caused Iovis to fall on his knees:

"She was my mother, and my birth certificate has your name on it."

Iovis wanted to think the woman in front of him was lying. The fact that Juno was her mother did not surprise him, the resemblance was so obvious, but that Iovis was her father couldn't possibly be true. Sure Juno and Iovis had been close during those few months they'd known each other, but that Juno would have gotten pregnant from just one time? Impossible... Or at least unlikely.

On the other hand, Juno had disappeared into thin air without an obvious explanation. About a year after her disappearance, Iovis had gotten a suspicious letter from Juno and the woman sitting in front of him right now looked about the right age...

Iovis needed proof and asked the woman for a permission to make a phone call to get it. Diana permitted it under the condition he doesn't tell his contact what's going on. Iovis took out his cell phone and selected the number of the best analyst he knew. If someone were to be found, Ceres Macbeth would find them.

***

Ceres Macbeth was browsing the cyberspace somewhere between national secrets and suspect's private lives as she heard the way too cheery ring-tone of her phone.

"Iovis! Good to hear from you too. How's Europe?" Ceres answered in her usual, informal manner.

"It was warmer in London. It's sleeting here in Helsinki. I need your help. I want you to find information about someone. It's personal so, please keep it a secret, OK?" Iovis asked. Ceres said she'll do anything as long as she gets a bar of Finnish chocolate as a souvenir. Iovis gave a laugh and said he was looking for a woman called Juno Sullivan.

Ceres' fingers started running across the keyboard at near the speed of light. Finding people was her speciality. Juno Sullivan, however, wasn't exactly what you'd call easy to find.

Juno wasn't the most common name in the world but it wasn't the rarest one either. She narrowed her search down based on age and physical features, but still couldn't find a match before including in her search the deceased.

"Let's see... Juno Sullivan. A Caucasian redhead, if she were alive she'd be about 39... Now this is curious..." Ceres mumbled.

As Iovis was being curious, Ceres explained that a woman matching the search criteria showed up on the map 21 years ago but neither a birth certificate nor a social security number existed from before that anywhere in North America.

The woman had been brought to a hospital it Ottawa where she gave birth to a daughter. Eleven years later she'd drowned in a boating accident where her daughter had been with her. The girl was never found.

Ceres was about to ask what this was all about, but Iovis hung up before she could. Driven by curiosity, Ceres dug out the birth certificate of Juno's daughter before erasing the search results from existence. It answered her question.

"What's your name?" Iovis asked Black Iris as he ended the call.

"Diana Sullivan", Diana said and gave a laugh right after: "Funny. The only person alive who knows my name is the one who wants me behind bars." Iovis didn't look amused.

Next, Iovis asked Diana how she'd survived the boating accident that took her mother's life. Iovis could guess the answer he'd get and it was giving him the chills.

"Do you want the long version or the short one?" Diana asked and Iovis said he wasn't in a hurry to go anywhere. So Diana told him everything, starting from the beginning. All about who Juno really was, what she'd raised her daughter into, why she did that, and how she'd met her end at the hands of her own child.

"Now that I think about it, I don't believe mom wanted to do that to me. I remember vaguely hearing her often cry herself to sleep. But back then I was so blinded by hatred I couldn't see the whole picture and obeying her last order was easy. Now I wish I'd finished myself off instead", Diana finished her story.

Iovis, who had at some point sat down, needed a few minutes to digest the information blast he'd just received. Juno had been an assassin the whole time? It explained a lot. Why Juno had shown up in his neighbourhood at that time, why she'd been so interested in Iovis' family, why she'd suddenly disappeared, and last but not least, why Iovis' father had been gunned down during his election speech a month after Juno's disappearance.

Iovis didn't want to believe that the seventeen year old girl who'd stolen his heart, him being the same age as her, had only been using him to get to his father. However, the horrific images Iovis was coming up with disappeared as Diana opened her mouth:

"Juno didn't kill your father. Luckily the reports of the case had not yet been destroyed so I managed to get access to them. With them the course of events was easy to figure out."

"The assassination of your father was supposed to be a secret one, meaning it was meant to look like an accident or a natural death, so Juno studied his routines day and night in order to figure out how to finish the job. During that observation period she probably ran into you and decided to use you to her advantage. You were the same age so no one would be suspicious seeing you two together."

"However, as she was pretending, her attention switched from your father to you and she totally forgot why she was there. She fell in love with you and let your relationship go too far. When she realized it, she decided to protect you the best she could and disappeared out of your life, reporting to the Organization that the job was a failure. At that moment the status of the assassination changed from secret to open and another assassin was sent to finish the job."

In a way Iovis felt relieved after hearing that but at the same time he felt a certain level of guilt. He had a wife and a child and now he found out he had an adult daughter whose existence he'd known nothing about. If he'd known, would things have been different?

"I don't understand why Juno couldn't just trust me. If I'd known I would have..." Iovis couldn't finish the sentence as Diana interrupted him:

"Done what? Helped her? How? A teenage couple versus a worldwide organization of contract killers. Even a child would be able to tell how that would end. If Juno had trusted you then, you would both be dead by now. The only reason why I do now what she couldn't do then is that the circumstances have changed. You are working on the right side of the law for a worldwide organization and can actually do something now."

Diana was right. Hindsight doesn't help anyone, especially when things could only have gotten worse. The only thing that could be done now, was clean up.

"Diana..." Iovis said while placing his hand on her shoulder, "I must be out of my mind and my superiors are going to be so angry at me but... I am going to help you. Just tell me what I need to do."

Chapter 7.

"I've caught Black Iris." That was the most beautiful phrase Apollo Franco had ever heard. However, it was followed by a sentence no one in the leading ranks of Interpol ever wanted to hear: "She wants to make a deal."

There was nothing strange about criminals themselves in requesting a deal, but this was about a person who had killed in twenty different countries and against whom there was no circumstantial evidence. A confession would be the only way to get a conviction, but not many nations would be willing to make a deal with the accused in order to get it. The charges were that serious.

The conditions of the person calling themselves Black Iris were clear. She wanted to be convicted of *all* her crimes in one trial, in Finland, and according to Finland's laws. In return she'd confess to everything officially and give a lot of valuable information that would mean bad times for other criminals like her. But the deal was All-Or-Nothing. No deal, no confession, no information... No conviction.

Apollo didn't know if he himself would be willing to make a deal like that with a murderer who'd killed hundreds of people, and he knew there were nations that definitely would not be. Many would think a conviction in Finland would be way too lenient. On the other hand it was better than nothing...

After contemplating for a moment Apollo told Iovis he'd agree to arrange an international meeting where the fate of Black Iris would be decided. Iovis' job would be to keep an eye on the suspect and inform the

Finnish police force. Apollo would take care of the rest. Now the case was completely in God's hands.

***

"Is this really necessary?" Diana asked, pointing with her finger at the handcuffs Iovis had used to chain them to each other. "I'm not going to run away."

"Until we get to the assembly place it is. After that you'll have to wait a while handcuffed in the interrogation room", Iovis answered. The handcuffs were completely unnecessary (and useless), but the leaders had insisted on it.

Sitting in the back of a police car Diana could do nothing but look out of the window and pray. She'd taken a huge risk. Were the plan to fail, she and everyone she'd been involved with would be facing the full wrath of the Organization. Nonetheless, she knew she was doing the right thing. Maybe for the first time in her life.

The location chosen for the assembly was the building used by the City Council of Tampere. It was secure enough location wise and had everything that was needed: An assembly space and, for interrogation, rooms that could be locked from the outside.

In a way, Diana found it amusing that someone thought they could get anything useful out of her in a legal (or illegal) interrogation without agreeing to her demands first.

When they'd arrived at the designated place, they didn't stay to observe the curve appeal of the building and went straight inside. All the representatives had found their way to the location, so the meeting began right after Diana had been taken to the interrogation room reserved for her.

"Sterling, are you out of your mind!?" the USA representative yelled at him after hearing the demands. "There's no way those demands could be accepted!" All other representatives agreed. Iris had killed too much to get that good a deal. Especially for the representatives of countries with a death penalty in use, a conviction in Finland was as good as an amnesty.

Iovis sighed. He had expected that response and now he'd have to convince the twenty representatives and leaders of countries that they had no choice in the matter.

"We have neither eye witnesses nor circumstantial evidence against her and she's stated she'll officially confess if and only if we agree to her demands. Under the circumstances, it won't matter what country the trial will be held in. She'd be released immediately due to the lack of evidence, she'd be assassinated for betrayal and someone else would take her place in no time at all."

"I'm not insane, I'm being realistic. This is the only way to both get the conviction and stop a successor from taking her place. We can stop the murders caused by that organization and a conviction given here is still better than nothing", Iovis spoke while silently praying that everything would go according to plan.

The audience stayed silent as Iovis' words hit the nail on the head. The only person the Iris had admitted their identity to, was Iovis Sterling and that conversation had not been recorded. Everything Iris had to do to get away with everything, was to deny having said anything to Iovis.

The representatives debated amongst themselves for hours. Some left the conference room for a moment to make a call to the leader of their country and, one by one, they all agreed to the demands of the unyielding assassin. All except the representative of the United States of America. He was still of the opinion that Iris deserved the death penalty. Still, he didn't wish for that mysterious "Organization" to continue its existence...

The representative demanded to speak to the suspect himself. He was one of the best interrogators in his country and was certain he'd get the suspect to spill the beans.

Oh how complicated this had become... The interrogation would be a waste of time and Iovis knew it. However, it wasn't his decision to make and the representative got permission to go interrogate the suspect and see if he could get anything out of her.

***

If you think you know what agonizing boredom is, think about making a two hour car drive in a quiet company, only to then be shut in a ten square meter (just over 100 square feet) room with no windows for hours, with no possibility for reading, drawing, crafting, gaming or any other form of entertainment.

Diana knew that feeling way too well. During that time, she hadn't even had anything to eat. She was lucky to even be able to go to the bathroom when necessary and even that had to be done handcuffed to the guard... Right now she could give almost anything for a sandwich and a hand-held game console with a game...

The silence was broken by a door slamming open, and a man Diana didn't know stepped in. She knew immediately her demands had not been accepted. She fixed her gaze into a spot next to the door and kept it locked there as the man began to speak. Diana did not want to talk to him.

Her thoughts wandered between heaven and earth and she didn't hear a word the man was saying. The interrogator could tell the woman was being absent but couldn't do anything to get her attention no matter how hard he tried. One couldn't help but admire that power of concentration.

After two hours of wasted effort the man had no choice but to give up and return to other representatives. At that, before returning to the assembly hall he made a phone call to the President of his country. With the permission from the President, the USA representative would sign a deal with Black Iris and the woman would be convicted in Finland according to Finland's laws.

***

The bell rang a whole different tone when Iovis stepped into the interrogation room with papers, signed by the representatives of twenty different countries. Iovis had also brought something the woman had been dieing for for way too long.

"Iovis, you're a life saviour!" Diana exclaimed as she got started on the packed sandwiches he'd brought for her. Never before had convenience food tasted so good.

"How did it go?" she asked with a mouth full of food. Iovis replied with a phrase they'd agreed on beforehand that expressed the deal had been accepted:

"They may not be as obvious nowadays, but the time for miracles is not over yet."

Iovis set the papers down in front of her so she could read them herself. There was only one signature missing from them and it belonged to Diana. Iovis pointed at the line before the signatures to guide Diana's attention to it.

"They accepted your demand but only by being allowed to add one of their own", he said.

Diana read the line and smiled. Apparently information alone wasn't enough for the nations. They wanted Diana to help take down the Organization personally and on the front lines. The demand was not unreasonable. On the contrary it was a sensible action. Diana wasn't trying to set a trap for the law enforcers but they didn't know that. Demanding her to the front lines was expected.

Diana read the contract once more to make sure the demands she'd set had not been change and that nothing had been left out. After finishing, she took a pen into her hand, found the space reserved for her signature and signed it with her real name: Diana Sullivan.

Diana took out a stick of lip balm and handed it to Iovis saying:

"Don't let appearances fool you. There's a flash card embedded in the base. It contains all you need to know."

Iovis took the stick and said he'd send the information on it to his analyst right away. After that Diana wrote an official confession and signed it. The easiest part was now over.

Iovis was about to go deliver the papers and the data when he decided to ask just one more question. At the end of the day, there was still one thing bothering him.

"How did you find out about my family and background?" Iovis asked. Diana replied with a single sentence:

"I know a good information broker from Tokyo." Iovis knew right away who Diana was referring to. There was no need to ask more.

*"Murder is unique in that it
abolishes the party it injures, so
that society must take the place of
the victim, and on his behalf
demand atonement or grant forgiveness."*
W.H. Auden

*The final judgement, be it conviction
or forgiveness, will always be in the hands of God.
All we can do in life is choose
what is best for society, and that choice
should be made based on
how likely the criminal is to re-offend.*

Chapter 8.

This is a good opportunity to work in some more background information about the Organization. As stated before, the Organizations sole purpose is to kill people for money. If one wants someone dead and they have at least ten thousand dollars worth extra money, the Organization will do the job for them no questions asked, and even with a cause of death of the client's choice.

However, they could reject the job request if the required murder conditions are impossible or too specific, or if they demand the contract killer to commit suicide. Nonetheless, it doesn't mean the employees of the Organization are irreplaceable. All 44 Organization employees: 13 contract killers/assassins, 12 public contacts, a 15 person base maintenance team, 3 computing specialists and the leader himself, were all replaceable if necessary.

Although only a handful of the employees were officially contract killers and assassins, all Organization employees had gone through the same upbringing and could seamlessly be transferred from one job to another.

There were no friendships, and loyalty had everything to do with how well someone did their job.

The Organization had five fixed bases and dozens, if not hundreds, small safe houses all over the world that changed constantly. Normally all 44 employees were scattered all over the world across all 5 bases, but there was one day in the year when everyone temporarily put their jobs aside and assembled in one single base: First of May, also known as the annual meeting.

The purpose of the annual meeting was to go through the achievements of every employee and make sure everyone's loyalties lay in the Organization and only the Organization.

If someone failed to attend the annual meeting they were labelled as a traitor, with no exceptions, and those attending who were suspected of betrayal were exposed to a third degree using anything but legal methods. The annual meeting was also the time when the Organization was at its most vulnerable.

Diana's reasons to attend the annual meeting this year were different from the usual ones. This year's meeting was to be held in the Los Angeles base and Diana had, together with the FBI, conducted a plan to give the Organization hell.

The agents wouldn't be able to get inside the base on their own, so Diana was meant to open the doors (emergency exits) for them from the inside. The emergency exits were unsupervised so the law enforcers would be able to enter from there unnoticed. The FBI would also have a team watching the main entrances so that no one would get out.

The main entrance was basically the same as that of the Southampton base and the security system was about the same. Getting in didn't cause any problems for Diana.

She breathed a sigh of relief as the lift began to move. Everything was ready. All she'd have to do is wait for the remaining members of the Organization to arrive, and leave the group using a believable excuse to open the emergency exits. Everything was going well. Maybe a bit too well.

Diana had barely made it two steps out of the lift as she heard a familiar, ominous sound next to her ear. It was the sound of the safety being released from a Sig Sauer.

"I didn't think I'd ever see this day come", Nigel Ramirez, real name Mercurius Garcia, said while pressing the barrel against the temple of the red haired woman.

"I always thought you were reliable but my ears have heard a news saying you've betrayed the Organization. Is that true?"

The tone in Nigel's voice was chilling and Diana couldn't help but wonder who was the rat. It had to be someone among the Interpol, the representatives, and the countries' leaders. No one else could know both how to contact the Organization and that Diana had switched sides.

She had been pushed between the rock and the hard place. If she admitted to being a traitor she'd be shot here and now. But if she denied the rumours, she'd be suspected of lying and tortured half to death. Her position in front of her boss couldn't get any more disadvantageous.

"Nigel... What makes you think I could betray the Organization? This job may not exactly be legal but it's the only thing I can do well", Diana lied. The best she could do now was stall for time for as long as possible.

Mercurius wanted to believe Iris. Nonetheless, he could not be sure about anything anymore. He found it best to reveal something about his source:

"One of my former clients contacted me and was... Let's just say... Concerned for his own head. His contract may have had nothing to do with you, but it doesn't mean you couldn't have handed over information regarding it to the Interpol together with the rest of the data you gave them. I have no idea how you got it out of the building but..." Nigel sighed.

"Iris, Iris, Iris... We all thought we could at least trust the best in our business. But it's over now. I wish I could believe you but the allegations are just too serious. However, I'm sure we'll find someone just as good in no time. Sayonara."

Diana tried to react and move away from the gut before it would go off but was a fraction too slow. Nigel pulled the trigger at the same second he said the last vowel of the word "sayonara".

***

Diana had had more luck on her side on that day than in her entire career as a contract killer. Mercurius' trusty Sig Sauer jammed and all that could be heard from a shot was a pathetic click.

The leader of the Organization hadn't yet recovered from the shock lasting a fraction of a second as Diana had already taken advantage of the situation, kicked her boss where the sun doesn't shine, and grabbed his gun before rushing towards the stairs, and running down towards the emergency exits as fast as she could. Only part of the Organization was present in the building, but that was better than nothing.

Chased by a rain of bullets, Diana opened the emergency exits and ran past the FBI troops waiting on the other side of the doors, saying the plan had been compromised but the operation would still continue to the end. The men did as they were told as Diana travelled through the tunnel towards the exit.

Chapter 9.

If Diana's thoughts were to be written down now, every other word would have to be censored. Her cover had been blown and now they'd have to make up a new plan to catch the rest of the Organization; to catch those who weren't inside the base.

She was supposed to meet up with Iovis at a prearranged location and move on to a safe-house from there, but her road was cut short before she had the chance.

A young, perhaps 14-year-old, blond girl was standing in front of her. She recognized her from the employee files she'd downloaded: Venus Ambrose. According to the records, she was the most likely successor to Black Iris.

Before the start of the operation Diana had explained to the law enforcers that the adult members of the Organization should be shot first and questioned later. They'd show no mercy and one shouldn't show it to them, or they'd end up paying for it with their lives. The children and the youth were a bit different.

Even though they too were merciless killers, they may still have a small spark of hope left in them. Hope in that they could one day escape from their fate with that cursed profession. They hadn't chosen it and few wanted to go along with it forever.

Venus looked right at Diana with her forest green eyes. The women observed each other for a second before they simultaneously took out their handguns and pointed them at each other. Only one thing was showing on Venus' face: disappointment.

"Why are you doing this? You can't escape the Organization", Venus asked.

They could have shot each other then and there, but they both waited. Both wanted to hear what the other had to say.

"Whether I get away or not, I don't care one way or another. I just want to do what's right for once", Diana said, paused for a moment, and continued:

"The Organization's going to take a lot of damage because of this. Even if you shoot me now you can't save the Organization. I may not be able to escape but neither can they. The Organization is doomed so why not just give up?"

Just thinking about the words "giving up" brought a bad taste into Venus' mouth. Giving up would mean either suicide or a death penalty. Venus wasn't ready to face death just yet. Truth be told, death was the only thing the girl feared truly and openly.

Diana saw her doubts and tried to calm her down:

"Don't be scared. You're still young and Interpol, FBA, CIA, MI7... Heck, all the alphabets know your story. If you give yourself in, you'll be looked at as a victim of the circumstances. You'd get away with a slap on the wrist."

The girl's gun-holding hand started to shake. She didn't know if it had something to do with what Iris said or that she'd kept her hand in that position for a bit too long.

"Why are you doing this?" Venus asked again. "You were the most capable, the most cold blooded killer of all. You could have continued for all eternity without getting caught. What changed?" The girl didn't understand the woman's motivation to work with the police.

Diana smiled with a smile so gentle it didn't suit the face of a killer. Her answer to the girl's question was short and sweet: "I found God."

Venus chuckled as she heard it, so Diana thought it best to clarify:

"The whole story is so strange you wouldn't believe me if I told you everything. One thing lead to another and soon I met a young pastor. At first I thought he was moonstruck but he knew what he was talking about, be it science, theology, apologetics, or the core message of Christianity."

"He told me about God and Jesus Christ. At first I didn't understand but I soon realized it was all true. There is a God and he sent his only begotten Son into the world to pay for our sins so that none who believe in him would have to try to do the impossible and redeem themselves."

"There is no greater love than being ready to give one's own life for someone else. We all should understand that." Diana put down her gun and reached her hand out to the girl.

"I'm not worried about death anymore. The first step of faith isn't as big as it looks. Believe in what He has done for you and he will save you from the posthumous Hell. Take my hand and through me He will help you for as long as you still live on Earth. Nothing is stopping you. He wants to be on your side and all you have to do is let Him", Diana said in a calm voice.

Venus didn't understand. Could you be saved through faith? No concrete actions? Nothing but faith? It sounded too easy to be true. And what came to God's existence? Venus was ready to deny it then and there, but then she considered the situation a bit more carefully.

Iris had lived a life not too different from Venus and been just as sceptical about the other side. Still, she'd managed to find something that convinced her of not only that there was a God, but also that God is good. If Iris could do it, could Venus too?

"Iris..." Venus was about to say something when Diana interrupted:
"Forget that title the Organization gave me. My name is Diana. Use that."

"D... Diana... I..." Venus put down her gun and reached out towards Diana's hand.

At the moment their fingers were barely touching, Venus fell to the ground, lifeless, and Diana felt sharp pain in her upper arm. What had just happened? Diana hadn't heard a shot... A sniper!!!

Diana escaped to a nearby alley, away from the sight of the sniper's scope as fast as she could. She was leaning against the wall while putting pressure on her wound, cursing silently in her mind. She'd been so close... If she'd only taken into consideration that someone from the Organization was observing the area from a distance with a rifle, this could have been avoided.

The ambush had been so obvious Diana couldn't help but blame herself for not even considering it, and the girl had paid for it with her life. She hadn't deserved it.

Diana hadn't had the time to sink any deeper into self-reproach as she saw movement at an alley on the other side of the street. It was Iovis and he was moving towards his daughter. Diana didn't want to see one more person die because of her.

"Sniper!" she shouted as loud as she could so that Iovis couldn't not hear it. Anyway, Iovis didn't even slow down. Was he out of his mind? If he were to get shot...

Diana closed her eyes so she wouldn't have to watch her father die. But the terrifying thing didn't happen, and soon Diana felt the warmth of a hand gently landing on her right shoulder.

"Don't worry. Lady Luck wasn't on the Organization's side and a civilian heard the shot. A squad arrived there in no time at all. I heard from my radio just now that the sniper had been caught and cuffed", Iovis was consoling Diana, asking if she was alright, pointing at the gun shot wound.

"The bullet just scratched the surface. I'm fine... But..." Diana replied and reluctantly looked at the young girl's body.

"She was just about to give herself in when..." Diana was trying to explain but the words refused to come out of her mouth.

Iovis didn't need words to understand. He brought his radio to his mouth and explained to the operation leader that the sniper they'd caught just now had shot a girl, wounding Diana in the process.

After hearing that the reinforcements were on their way to their location, he put down his radio and said to Diana:

"There are still twelve members of the Organization on the loose but it won't take long for them to get caught. Their photo's have been sent to all the airports and border controls. They no longer have anywhere to run. It's over." Hearing those two words was like lifting a heavy weight off of Diana's shoulders. It's over.

Diana leaned against the wall and, for the fist time in years, relaxed. She was feeling a little tired but it did not bother her. She was free. Besides, the gunshot wound that had a moment ago been stinging like crazy had slowly become numb. But Iovis wasn't relieved to hear Diana mention it. On the contrary.

Iovis took a closer look at Diana's wound and what he saw caused him to get worried for real. It wasn't just a scratch and she had lost a considerable amount of blood.

He took out his radio once more and demanded the reinforcements to hurry up. There was no time to waste. Diana Sullivan had just lost her consciousness.

Chapter 10.

"God must have really been on your side", Iovis said to his daughter. They had just left the hospital where Diana had received a blood transfusion and her wound had been sown shut. Her life had been in danger but she'd pulled through.

While they had been in the hospital, eight more Organization members had been caught. Diana had kept her end of the bargain and the number of contract killings should go down at least for a while. Now there was only one thing left to do.

"When's the flight?" Diana asked. She'd soon be returning to Finland for her trial. What was waiting for her was most likely twenty years to a life in prison but it was still a lot better than being executed.

"Soon. I have already bought the tickets. I'll come with you to the trial and testify for you. You may be guilty of many wrongdoings but your actions in the last few days should still count for something", Iovis answered.

Diana wanted to say he didn't have to, but she still appreciated the gesture. The flight would be long and troublesome and hardly worth the effort. Having friendly company there felt good, even though Iovis was technically just escorting her to prison.

***

The spring's first lightning was flashing in the sky during the trial. The air was heavy and the atmosphere inside the court room was no lighter. The tribunal of Finland was under a lot of pressure when the responsibility of judgement of the world's most wanted criminal, Black Iris, was placed on their shoulders.

Diana had confessed so the usual step of hearing out witnesses (although Iovis had kept his word and testified for her) and long discussion periods over guilt and innocence were not needed. The guilt was clear. Now all that was left was to decide on an appropriate sentence.

It's needless to say most of the jury thought that a life in prison was the only punishment fitting the crime within the limits of Finnish law that would not stir up the anger of the nations involved. Many would have gladly decided on a death sentence had it been possible, but the laws of Finland forbade it.

Just as the judge was ready to pass judgement, a man sitting in the front row stood up and requested permission speak. That man's presence in the court room was not the most common thing but nor was it unheard of. He held a title that was appreciated, even though it didn't grant him much power within the borders of his country. He was the President of the Republic of Finland.

The judge allowed the President to speak. The man took out a stack of papers he had signed and said something unexpected:

He said he was going to use his power as the President to pardon Diana Sullivan.

At that moment the whole room came alive. Those present could not comprehend the man's decision nor had Diana expected it. The judge had to demand silence by hitting the stand with his hammer for the room to quiet down.

Considering that the nations demanded an explanation for his decision, the President explained that although Diana had killed hundreds of people, her latest actions had saved thousands. Her actions had been brave, even heroic, and deserved at least some sort of recognition. Because giving her a medal would be insane, clearing up her criminal record was the least he could do for her.

People still didn't want to make sense out of the President's logic but they eventually had to accept his crazy sounding decision. Diana would walk out of the court room a free woman and could without worries go wherever she wanted. As soon as a mountain of paperwork was finished. First of all she'd have to be officially brought back to life, and second of all, she didn't have a passport under her own name.

When Diana stepped outside with Iovis, the storm had already subsided, and the air smelled like ozone. The Sun's rays were shining through the layer of clouds that had just a moment ago been incredibly thick, as if to congratulate her.

Diana didn't know if she should be laughing or crying. She was free, but she had no place to go, and no idea what she should do next.

"Why do you look so serious?" Iovis asked. Diana told him all about her worries, and Iovis placed his hand comfortingly on her shoulder.

"You'll find your way sooner or later. Until then, you can come stay with me. Minerva will understand as soon as I explain who you are. Without the whole *formerly the world's most wanted criminal'* thing. Your identity as Black Iris shall remain a worldwide secret", Iovis said.

"And your son?" Diana wanted to accept the offer but didn't want to intrude if her own half brother wouldn't accept her.

"Mars? He'll get used to you. If you like video games you'll get along even better", Iovis assured.

Diana gave a laugh at her father's last comment. It may just be a modern day phenomenon or there was at least one thing among them that was genetic.

"Are you kidding? I love video games", Diana exclaimed. The duo laughed for a moment, in a way amused by the situation, and then moved on to enjoy the things Helsinki had to offer. They had time.

It would take a few weeks to return her to the books of the living and getting a passport could take months. As soon as she'd been brought back to life, she'd get an expedited passport she could use to return to Canada with her father. After that, her old life would officially be over.

Chapter 11.

The road from the nearest airport in Canada to Iovis' house was surprisingly long. He didn't live at the very centre of the city but further away at the edge of the suburbs. His house was a white, two-storied, three bedroom detached, and had all the necessary mod cons and a little extra.

When Iovis had called his wife, it was surprising how easily she had accepted it all. In a way normal to women, Minerva had been a little jealous after hearing about her husband's teenage romance, but she eventually let it go. After all, it happened long before they had even met.

Mars hadn't shown any particular excitement for his half sister but was sure to warm up to her in no time. The boy would still be at school at the time of their arrival, so he'd have to wait a little longer than his mother to meet the new family member.

"We're home", Iovis sighed as he parked his car on his own driveway. It had been forever since he'd last been home, and now he was going to get to spend a little more time there.

Diana didn't quite feel like she was home, but on the other hand it was her first time in that part of Canada. She'd get accustomed to it in no time. Truth be told, she was more worried about the other residents of the house than her not starting to feel at home soon.

Getting out of the car, Diana grabbed the bag containing all her belongings from the back seat. It was mostly clothes. Among them were also a couple of books, a hand-held game console and some games.

She didn't have a Bible but the thought of using blood money to buy one didn't feel quite right to her.

Iovis showed Diana around his home and offered her a former guest room to use, which his wife had prepared especially for her. Diana put down her bag and fell on the bed. She was so tired from the trip she just wanted to rest for a while.

"After I've gotten some rest I'll start looking for a job right away. I don't want to be a mooch", Diana said.

"A job? Don't you have a nice pension fund stashed away on some off shore account?" Iovis wondered. Diana chuckled.

"I'm not gonna lie. You're right. I still wish to avoid using that blood money as much as possible", she explained.

Iovis understood completely what his daughter meant. She was a changed woman and it would be wrong to demand her to make use of the pieces from her past.

Iovis decided he too could use some rest and moved to the living room, leaving Diana alone. He sat on the sofa and turned on the television. There was nothing interesting airing on any of the channels, but he left the sports channel on just because.

It was hard to explain what he was feeling at that moment. Imagine that for years you've been trying to achieve something and when you finally do, the circumstances are anything but what you were expecting.

Meeting Diana had awoken many suppressed memories and opened old wounds. Iovis couldn't stop thinking about his first love, Juno. The woman had appeared in his life out of nowhere and disappeared just as quickly, only to return to him in the form of their daughter.

At least now Iovis could move on with his life knowing exactly what had happened to her and where she was right now. Diana had revealed to him the location of Juno's grave and he was planning on making a visit there one day, together with his only daughter.

Juno... Wonder if it ever occurred to her that Iovis and Diana might cross paths some day? Perhaps not... Or maybe... Wait a minute!

Iovis jumped up from the sofa like it was on fire. He ran into the office and started going through his drawers. No... No... Not that either... Found it!

The man grabbed an open envelope from the drawer and took out of it another, smaller envelope. It was sealed and had never been opened. On the back of it, there was a riddle Iovis couldn't figure out for twenty years, but now the answer was obvious.

Iovis ran to the door of Diana's room and knocked before entering.

"What is it?" Diana asked. She was a bit concerned about the fact that he had been running. It usually didn't mean good.

Iovis sat next to his daughter on the bed and started to speak.

"I'd forgotten about this for twenty years... A year after Juno disappeared I got a letter from her. She assured that she loved me and apologized about having disappeared so suddenly, urging me to not look for her. Needless to say, I did not listen. It took me three years to finally give up."

"But that's not why I'm telling you this. The thing is that this came with the envelope", Iovis explained, handed Diana the envelope, and continued:

"In her letter, Juno forbade me from opening that. She said I would know whom it was addressed to as soon as I'd meet them. I think she meant you."

Diana took the envelope, although she could not fully take in what had just been said. How did Iovis know whom the letter was addressed to? Diana read the riddle on the back of the envelope and understood right away.

"The illegitimate child of the king, the father of gods,
wanders alone in the moonlight,
hunting souls, not knowing of their father,
baring the name of the queen."

"Iovis" was derived from the name "Jupiter" who in Roman mythology was, like Zeus in Greek mythology, the supreme God and the father of many Gods. By an illegitimate child, she was referring to Diana, whose father Iovis was, but whose parents had not been married. The "wandering in moonlight" and "hunting" were references to Diana's name, for "Diana" was the roman goddess of hunting and also the moon goddess together with Luna.

"Hunting" was also referring to Diana's profession as a contract killer. "Not knowing of their father" meant that Juno had no intention on telling Diana who her father was.

Jupiter being the king naturally made his wife, Juno, the queen. By "queens name" Juno was referring to her last name, as well as her role as Diana's mother.

Diana hesitated for a moment, but she wanted to know what Juno had to say to her. She opened the envelope and read her mother's last message to her:

"Diana, darling.

If you're reading this, you have most likely met Iovis. He's a good man and also your father. I can only hope that you two met under favourable circumstances considering your situation.

It is also possible that when you're reading this I am already dead, most likely by your hand. I do not deserve your forgiveness, but if you can find it in your heart, I am sorry. It was not my will to raise you a killer.

My intention was to carry you to term in secret, and then take you to your father's family, but fate stepped in and the labour began as I was on a mission with another assassin. I am truly sorry. If only I had been able to carry you for a week longer, everything would have bee better.

I already hate myself for what I'll have to do to you. God alone can forgive me for that.

My greatest wish now is that you'll be able to do what I couldn't. That you'll be able to escape that cursed Organization that ruins people's lives. If you could live a normal life, I would be satisfied. If you could also find God like I did, I could not be any happier.

I do not know if you can believe me when I say this but I guarantee you, this is true. I love you so much and will always love you till the time comes for you to take my life, and I'll still love you long after that.

Juno Sullivan"

Tears were gathering in Diana's eyes as she read the letter.

"Mom, you idiot... Of course I forgive you... And... I have done everything you wished... I should be the one to apologize. I hated you and didn't realize that you loved me... That you loved me so much you gave your life for me..." Diana said from among the tears.

Iovis wrapped his arm gently around Diana. To the both of them, this was the beginning of a new life.

Epilogue

That is how Diana Sullivan's story ended... No... That's how the life of Diana Sterling, my life, began. During the process, I took my father's last name.

A year has passed sense I moved in with my father. His wife welcomed me with open arms, but my little brother took a while to get used to my presence. Nonetheless, I soon became his best buddy after playing video games with him.

I quickly found myself a job from a local church and I haven't used my blood money for my own gain since then. Everything I had I gave away to churches for missionary work and humanitarian aid.

However, I have not fully severed my ties to the criminal world. Due to my past, the law enforcement agencies from many countries sometimes ask for my help with their tougher cases. I'm glad to help them, but I never want to touch firearms again.

I still live with Iovis and Minerva but I spend most of the year out on mission fields helping people and changing their lives for the better. Soon I'll be returning to the mission fields again.

"Are you leaving again? Which part of the world will you be going to this time?" dad asked. I answered I was going to Kenya while, at the same time, working on my computer. Iovis put his hand down on my shoulder.

"Let me guess... Neifion is going there?" he asked, and was right. Neifion Yates is the pastor of a local church and does missions work all around the world. We met eight months ago at a service and have been inseparable ever since.

"Life's unfair isn't it? I just got back my little girl and I already have to give her to another man", Iovis said suggestively.

"Dad!" I exclaimed while amused. I was no longer a little girl, but he still treated me like one from time to time. I wonder if all fathers are like that with their daughters?

And the Organization? Within two months of the initial attack against it, all the members were either arrested or shot while resisting arrest. All those who died in battle got a proper funeral. If you ask me, it was the least they deserved.

"Ask, and it shall be given you; seek, and ye shall find; knock, and it shall be opened unto you". Answers to the greatest questions and a road to a desired life are waiting to be discovered. Anyone can find it. They just need to seek. Although, sometimes one might need a little help.

My life was changed by one of my victims: The priest I shot in cold blood. He had already forgiven me before I had even wronged him, and his prayer revealed to me what I had unknowingly been searching for the whole time. His last prayer brought an angel to my side and he changed my life for better, for good.

People sometimes say to me that it was just a collection of coincidences and an active imagination. Some even call me mentally ill, but I know better. What I experienced was real and I wouldn't trade it for anything. I wouldn't go so far as to say that everything is perfect now, but I have woken up from

the twenty year long nightmare, and now, I feel alive.
Thanks be to God.

Printed in Great Britain
by Amazon

13751486R00057